INDIA FIRST:
Modern Parables of Peace and Patriotism

Commemorating 75 years of Indian Independence

Ramendra Kumar

Ukiyoto Publishing

All global publishing rights are held by

Ukiyoto Publishing

Published in 2022

Content Copyright © Ramendra Kumar

ISBN 9789360493431

Cover Design: Aniket Kumar

All rights reserved.

No part of this publication may be reproduced, transmitted, or stored in a retrieval system, in any form by any means, electronic, mechanical, photocopying, recording or otherwise, without the prior permission of the publisher.

The moral rights of the author have been asserted.

This is a work of fiction. Names, characters, businesses, places, events, locales, and incidents are either the products of the author's imagination or used in a fictitious manner. Any resemblance to actual persons, living or dead, or actual events is purely coincidental.

This book is sold subject to the condition that it shall not by way of trade or otherwise, be lent, resold, hired out or otherwise circulated, without the publisher's prior consent, in any form of binding or cover other than that in which it is published.

www.ukiyoto.com

To Dr. Santosh Bakaya, the brilliant, multi-dimensional writer who has been my most indefatigable cheerleader in the best of times, as well as the worst of times.

CONTENTS

A Father & A Patriot .	1
The Question	9
Saare Jahan Se Achha....	14
The Real Hero	19
Patriotism	22
Kabir	27
The Promise	36
Time Pass Uncle	43
About the Author	*50*

A Father & A Patriot

Abbu, how come nanaji does Puja while ammi and you perform *namaaz*?"eight-year-old Muskaan asked her father Imtiaz Hussain. They were sitting in the balcony of their flat on a Sunday morning munching groundnuts - the year was 2025.

"Before I answer your question let me tell you a little story."

"Wow! That's great, but make it a long one," Muskaan said snuggling up to her father.

"Muskaan, you must have read in your General Knowledge book that India and Pakistan fought a war in the year 1999. Pakistani intruders had invaded Kargil and the Indian forces had beaten them back. For the Indians, the Kargil conflict was the toughest war they had fought since independence. The war brought to light many tales of heroism, courage and compassion. One such story is that of a Major who was called Major Tiger by his colleagues because he was very brave and fearless. This tale is about him and his love for a little girl..It is a story of a father and a patriot.

***

It was three in the morning and it was pitch dark all around. Major Tiger was leading his men up the slopes of Point 4130. This was one of the key peaks overlooking the Srinagar-Leh highway. His task was to capture it at any cost. It took the soldiers more than eight hours to inch their way up. Every few minutes a hail of bullets would greet them as the intruders, firmly entrenched on top, kept firing. When they neared the top from the east side they were ambushed by a band of enemy soldiers from the west. Caught between the firing from the top and the enemy attack from the left, Major Tiger's men fought on bravely. They managed to beat back the attackers who had ambushed them but at a cost of twenty men. Major Tiger now had only three men with him and the intruders on top were at least twenty. He decided to take a risk. He called the artillery on his radio and told them to shell the top, asking for the shells to land five metres from where he and his men lay. In normal circumstances this would have been considered suicidal, but the situation was by no means normal.

Under the cover of the artillery fire Major Tiger and his men stormed the enemy bunkers. Taken by surprise the enemy fell like nine pins. After a pitched battle when he looked around an hour later, he found he was alone. All his men had died fighting. There seemed to be no signs of intruders too. Major Tiger's battalion had won the peak but at a very heavy cost.

As he stumbled between corpses looking for any sign of life, he noticed a movement from the corner of his eye. In a flash he turned back and was just in time to ward of a frontal attack by an enemy soldier. The attacker's bayonet just missed slicing through Major Tiger's left shoulder. As his adversary tried to recover his balance Major Tiger swung his rifle and caught him on the head. The soldier staggered back. The two opponents then lunged at each other. His adversary's bayonet pierced Tiger Major's arm, while his own bayonet entered the enemy's stomach. Major Tiger withdrew his rifle and stepped back. He didn't want to kill the soldier. He wanted to take him alive so that later he would be able to get some information from him.

"Surrender or I'll finish you," he shouted.

"I'd rather die with dignity than surrender," his opponent snapped back and with blood oozing out of his stomach made a desperate lunge at Major Tiger. In an instant Major Tiger lifted his rifle and shot him through the heart. As the soldier fell in a heap on the rocky ground Major Tiger couldn't help but admire the courage of his brave adversary.

***

Later when he returned to the base camp and the bodies of the soldiers had been brought back Tiger Major went through the papers retrieved from the bodies of the enemy. The soldier who had challenged Tiger Major and fought so bravely was Captain Ejaaz Khan. In his pocket was a letter written in a childish scrawl and a photograph of a seven-year-old girl. She was slim, fair and was clad in a navy blue *salvar kameez*. She had bright blue eyes, a small perky nose and two tiny pig tails. Tiger Major stared at the photograph mesmerised. He just couldn't take his eyes off. The little girl looked exactly like his own Neha - his daughter who had died at the age of six, her head in his lap. How could he forget that black Wednesday more than eight years ago when a speeding car had claimed the lives of the two people he loved the most in the world - Neha and her mother Sanjana.....

He read the letter. It was in Urdu. Having learnt it as a third language in school he could read Urdu, though with a little difficulty.

"Dear Abbu,

This is my tenth letter to you but you have replied to only one. I hope you are getting all my letters. Abbu, I am so proud of you. None of my friends has a father in the Pakistan Army. Come back soon. I am waiting to hear how you fought the Indian soldiers and won the battle for Pakistan.

Abbu, Nikhat *khala* was telling that in Delhi you get beautiful bangles. When you reach Delhi can you buy for me six red, four green and two blue bangles.

Abbu, I feel very lonely without you. Everyday I keep asking Baba when you'll come home. Please take care of yourself. Abbu if anything happens to you I ....

I love you so much Abbu.

Your little *shahzadi*,

Ayesha."

Major Tiger tried his best to fight back the tears welling up in his eyes but he couldn't. The crumpled paper in his hand was wet as he read it again and again....

For the first time in his life, he felt a regret for having killed an enemy soldier.

***

A month later the hostilities ended and the dialogues between India and Pakistan resumed.

Gradually Kargil disappeared from the newspapers and to most people remained only a memory. Normalcy was restored in the relationship between India and Pakistan. Cricketing ties and cultural exchange programmes resumed between the two countries.

But for Major Tiger Kargil was still burning in his heart. And it would continue smouldering till he had achieved his mission. Over the last one year or so he had made desperate efforts to trace the whereabouts of Ayesha. He had contacted the Pakistan High Commissioner in India as well as the Indian Ambassador to Pakistan. After a lot of follow up his wish had been fulfilled. He was to meet Ayesha in Lahore. This was the first definite step in his mission.

Ayesha lived with her grandfather. Her mother had died when she was three.

The door was opened by an old man of around seventy. Behind him clutching his *kurta* was Ayesha. She looked much taller than she did in the photograph and prettier. But there was a certain sadness in her eyes - a reflection of the tragedy that had destroyed her life.

"Are you the Indian Major?"

"Yes, *salaam vaalekum*," he replied in Urdu.

"*Vaalekum salaam*. I am Ayesha's grandfather Mohammad Khan and this is Ayesha."

Ayesha smile shyly and did an elaborate adaab.

Major Tiger handed her a packet. "This is for you."

"What is it?"

"Open it and see."

She opened the packet. Inside were six red, four green and two blue bangles. Ayesha held the bangles in her hands and kept staring at them as tears flowed down her cheeks....

***

Ayesha and Major Tiger hit it off very well. It was almost as if they had known each other for years. Major Tiger planned to stay in Lahore for a week but he stayed for a month. Every day he would visit Ayesha and the two of them would spend time talking and laughing together. Mohammed Khan had never seen her laugh so freely since her father's death.

On the day he was leaving Major Tiger made his proposal.

"What? That is impossible. How can you even think of such a thing? She is a Muslim child how can she live in a Hindu house? Moreover, I cannot of dream sending her so far away to stay in Delhi. There is no question at all. When the Pakistan Government official told me that you were an Indian Major and you knew my son before the Kargil war, I thought you just wanted to see your friend's daughter. If I had known you had such ideas, I would never have allowed you to meet Ayesha," Mohammed Khan shouted, his face turning red with anger.

"Please Khan Saheb, calm down and try to understand. I lost my daughter Neha when she was Ayesha's age. I see my Neha in her. It is as if she has been reborn as Ayesha. Believe, me Ayesha will stay in my house as my daughter but she can continue to be a Muslim. Just think Khan Saheb, you are quite old; You have no relatives. What is going to happen to her after your death? Who will look after her?"

"The two of us are happy the way we are. I can take care of her. I have Allah's blessings he will look after Ayesha. Now you please go away."

"Okay, I am leaving. But I'll come back in a month's time. Please think it over. You can ask Ayesha what she wants. I am sure she will agree to come with me."

***

Exactly a month later Major Tiger was once again knocking on the door of Ayesha's house.

It was opened by Ayesha. She was delighted to see him. She gave him a tight hug.

"Baba has gone to the Masjid. He will be back soon," Ayesha said after they had sat down in the living room.

Major Tiger's heart was thumping. He was hoping against hope that Mohammed Khan would agree.

"Has your baba told you about...about your going with me?"

"Yes, he has. I would love to go to India and stay with you but I can't leave baba alone. He has no one else in the world."

Major Tiger was silent for sometime and then spoke quietly.

"Ayesha why don't we take baba along with us? The stationery shop he has can be sold off and the money invested. He can live a retired life with us. There is a Masjid right next to my house in Delhi. It will be very convenient for him."

Ayesha's eyes brightened. "Can....can baba really come with me?"

"Why not? I would love to take him along provided he has no problem."

When baba returned home, Ayesha told him about Major Tiger's proposal.

Mohammed Khan seemed quite surprised.

"Please Baba, please don't say no. I want to go with Major Chacha but I can't leave you here. Please agree no," she pleaded, climbing on to his lap and putting her little arms around him.

Mohammed Khan didn't answer for sometime.

Finally, after what seemed an eternity to Major Tiger he spoke, "Okay, if Ayesha wants it, I can't say no."

***

Shifting from Lahore to Delhi was not an easy task. But in six months Ayesha and baba were settled in Major Tiger's house which had now become their home.

Three years later baba passed away.

It was only when Ayesha was eighteen that Major Tiger whom she now called Major Abbu told her how her father had died.

She was shocked. Her face turned white and she started screaming at him. She called him a liar and a murderer. She threw herself on her bed and cried her heart out, refusing to even eat anything.

Major Tiger sat beside her patiently waiting for the shock, anger and agony to subside. Then he started slowly explaining to her. "Little one, both Captain Ejaaz Khan and I were only doing our duty. We were strangers fighting for our respective countries. It was just a chance that he died and I survived. It could have very easily been the other way around. Ayesha, in a war, on both sides there are only patriots and martyrs - there are no murderers. The real murderers are the politicians who unleash a war. It is they who should be accused of murder, not the brave soldiers who give up their lives or take other innocent lives for the sake of their motherland."

Gradually Ayesha got over the trauma. She realised what Major Abbu was telling was the stark truth. She once again started treating him with the same love, respect and admiration that she used to.

When she was twenty-one, she got married to a computer engineer working for a software company -"

"And his name is Imtiaz Hussain and he is my abbu," Muskaan squealed clapping her hands. "See Abbu, I guessed right. Ammi is

Ayesha and Major Tiger is my nanaji."

"Yes, my child. Now, do you know why your ammi and abbu go to the Masjid while your nanaji goes to the Mandir?"

"Yes, Abbu I know. But where should I go when I grow up?"

"Anywhere you want, my *shehzaadi*. All roads lead to God," Imtiaz Hussain said, giving Muskaan a warm hug.

The Question

Raghav lifted her up and was about to send her crashing to the ground when he heard her scream.

"Chachu!"

He froze and stared at her. Suspended in mid-air the slim and pretty ten-year-old was trembling.

"Its..me..Shahnaz...your Munni," she stammered, her eyes dilating with fear.

***

It was evening. Raghav was sitting in his house eating *paratha* and *achaar*. He was a truck driver who lived in a slum in the heart of Baroda. He had just returned from a trip to Ahmedabad.

"Chachu," he looked up.

Seven-year-old Munni was staring at him with tears in her eyes.

"What happened little one? Why are you crying?"

"Mini says she won't get her *gudda* married to my *gudiya*."

"Why?"

"Because my *gudiya* Salma is a Muslim and her *gudda* Kishan is a Hindu."

"Where is Mini? Call her."

A minute later Raghav's daughter Mini was standing in front, staring defiantly at him.

"Mini, why are you making Munni cry? Why can't your *gudda* marry Munni's *gudiya*?"

"Bapu, grandma was telling me there cannot be a marriage between a Hindu and a Muslim. So how can Kishan marry Salma?" Mini asked.

Raghav looked at her for couple of seconds searching for a suitable answer to her question. Then drawing her close he said, "Mini your grandma is old. During her time, it was not possible. Times have changed. Go ahead and marry your *gudda* with Munni's *gudiya*. And don't forget to tell me when the wedding is. I'll buy *jalebis* and distribute to all the *baratis*."

The two girls clapped their hands in glee and holding hands scampered out.

***

Munni's real name was Fatima. She was Raghav's neighbour Shauqat Ali's daughter. Shauqat worked in a textile mill. When a daughter was born to Raghav he had named her Mini. A month later when Shauqat was blessed with a girl Raghav had declared, "Shauqat bhai, if my daughter is Mini than her younger sister should be called Munni."

And so, the name had stuck. Hardly anyone called her Fatima. She was known only as Munni.

Mini and Munni grew up together and remained the best of friends. When the girls were seven Shauqat got a better job in another mill located in Ahmedabad. He shifted with his family to the city.

Mini and Munni cried their hearts out and promised to keep visiting each other. Mini made a couple of trips with her father to Ahmedabad and Munni came to Baroda once, but after that they lost touch.

***

Raghav looked at the girl. Yes, her face was familiar. It was Munni. He lowered her.

"Where is your abbu?"

"Chachu, they are all on the roof. Seeing a big crowd rushing every one ran up. Abbu was saying the crowd would burn the house. I slipped away and came down to collect my *gudiya*. I couldn't leave her, could I?"

There was a sound of footsteps. Raghav turned around. Kaaliya, Paresh, Vithal and Rana entered the house. Their faces were drenched in sweat and in their hands, they carried sticks and swords. Seeing them Munni hid behind Raghav, her face turning white.

"Come on Raghav what are you waiting for? Let's look for the infidels. They must be holed up like rats somewhere," shouted Kaaliya.

"No, Kaaliya there is no one here."

"What do you mean? Then where did this girl come from?" demanded Rana.

"Rana is right. They must be hiding on the roof," Vithal said and the group advanced.

"Stop!" Raghav shouted raising his arm. He was holding a sword, which glinted in the light. "You are not going anywhere. This is my friend Shauqat's house. We are not going to touch them."

"What do you mean this is your friend's house? In the train at Godhra they burnt alive 59 people - 40 of them were women and children," screamed Kaaliya.

"When our children were going up in flames did your friend come to the rescue?" demanded Vithal.

"Shut up!" thundered Raghav. "To reach them you'll have to tackle me first."

The four of them stared dumb struck. Raghav was tall and muscular. With his eyes red, his muscles taut and his face set, he looked menacing.

"*Chalo yaar*. If this fellow is willing to betray his religion for the sake of a Muslim let him. But we can't fight with some one of our own faiths simply because he is acting like a traitor," Kaaliya shouted and spitting in disgust turned back. The other men followed him out looking for a fresh quarry.

Raghav wiped the sweat from his forehead.

"Munni quickly take me to your father."

As Munni led him up the stairs, Raghav saw a man coming down. He recognised his friend Shauqat.

"Munni, where were you? Thank God –" Shauqat stopped in mid-sentence on seeing Raghav. "Raghav, so you have come to kill us?"

"No Abbu, Chachu saved our lives. He shouted at the other men and sent them away."

"Shauqat bhai, we don't have much time to lose. Let us go before the rioters return," Raghav said.

"But where *mian*. The whole of Ahmedabad is burning."

"You are right. Ahmedabad is not safe. We'll go to Baroda My truck is parked nearby. I'll take you home."

***

On the way Raghav told Shauqat the entire story. "As you know yesterday morning one of the compartments of the Sabarmati express was set on fire. All the 59 Hindus in it were burnt alive. In retaliation Hindus have started attacking Muslims in several parts of Gujarat. I too am a member of a Hindu organisation. I came to Ahmedabad in my truck along with several others. Since morning we have been moving from locality-to-locality smashing, burning and killing everyone in sight. Had I not seen Munni and recognised her I would have...." Raghav stopped and looked at Shauqat.

Munni who was sitting on Shauqat's lap spoke, "Chachu that day when Munni told that her grandma was objecting to a Muslim marrying a Hindu you had said, "Mini, your grandma is old. During her time, it was not possible. The times have changed and we have become modern now. But chachu if the times have changed and we have become modern why are Hindus and Muslims still killing each other?"

Raghav looked at the little girl. She was staring at him, her bright eyes, her innocent face asking a question which he wondered if he could ever answer.

Raghav reached out and gently patted Munni. "I can't really answer your question little one. But all I can say is that only when we adults start asking such questions to ourselves will this madness end."

As the truck left behind the old city of Ahmedabad, Raghav could see, in the rear-view mirror, the smoke from the burning buildings darkening the evening sky.

Saare Jahan Se Achha....

The Geetanjali Express came to a halt. Yogesh Kumar ran towards the AC first class compartment with his thirteen-year-old daughter, Varsha in tow. As Varsha watched, a thirty-five-year-old woman got down followed by a young boy, Varsha's age.

"Varsha, this is your mausi, Manisha Peters. And this handsome young man is your cousin Hari."

Varsha did a namaste to her aunt and held out her hand to Hari. As they shook hands Hari's tense face broke into a friendly grin.

"Nice meeting you Varsha," Hari said in heavily accented English.

Varsha's aunt Manisha was a computer professional in the U.S.A. She had married an American, Henry Peters who was a doctor. Manisha had come to India to attend a conference and had brought Hari along. This was Hari's first visit to India in ten years.

As they were driving home Varsha looked at her cousin who was sitting beside her and staring out of the window. Even though they were both the same age, Hari was almost half a foot taller.

As they chatted, Varsha found Hari was quite easy to talk to.

'I think I am going to like him and we are going to have a great time together," Varsha thought to herself.

When they reached home Varsha's mum and her daadi came out to welcome the guests.

Manisha bent down to touch daadi's feet."

"Why did mum bend down. Did she drop something?" Hari whispered.

"No, silly. Mausi bent down to touch my daadi's feet. In India we touch the feet of elders as a mark of respect to them."

"Who did you say the old lady was?"

"She is my daadi, my father's mother."

"Does she stay with you?"

"Of course! Why? Doesn't your daadi, I mean your grandma, stay with you?"

"No, she doesn't."

"Then she must be staying with your uncle or aunt?"

"No, she stays in an Old Age Home.

"Oh! How sad....." Varsha started saying and then bit her lip.

***

That evening after dinner Varsha told Hari, "Come let us go to daadi's room?"

"Why is there anything special?"

"She has a never-ending stock of fascinating stories."

"Really, let us go."

Daadi made them sit beside her and in her quaint old-fashioned English began telling then tales.

A couple of hours later when Manisha peeped in, she found daadi propped up in bed with Hari and Varsha, curled up on either side, fast asleep.

"Ammaji, should I....." Manisha started saying when daadi stopped her.

"Sh! Let them sleep," she said gently patting Hari on his head.

***

Next day Hari asked Varsha, "Does daadi tell you stories every day."

"Almost. I cuddle up with her every night and listen to her lovely tales. When I come home from school in the afternoon, she is always waiting for me with something hot and delicious. Even though my mum makes lunch before she leaves for work, the dessert is always made by daadi. You should eat her *gajar ka halva*, you'll never stop licking your fingers."

Hari was silent for some time.

"You know I too have working parents, but the big difference is I don't have a daadi waiting for me at home. I come home to an empty house, warm my food in the micro-wave, switch on the TV and eat with either NatGeo or Star Sports for company."

"What about dinner?"

"My parents usually come home late so I end up eating alone."

"In our house we have made it a practise to have dinner together. When papa or mum sometimes gets stuck in the office, they give us a tinkle and we wait for then. And we never switch on the TV while we are having dinner. Papa says dinner time is private and sacred and there should not be any disturbance. We keep sharing the day's happenings and laugh and joke with each other. It is all such fun."

***

It was Sunday evening and Manisha, Hari and Varsha were sitting in the living room. Monday early morning the guests were to take the train to Kolkota and from there they would be flying the same night to New York.

"Mum, yesterday when Varsha asked me to go to her school to witness the Annual Day celebration, I was reluctant. I thought I would get bored stiff. But you know I really enjoyed myself?"

"Really, that's great!" Manisha said.

"I learnt so many new things. Almost all of Varsha's friends can read, write and speak three languages and some even four and five. Isn't it amazing? Back home most of us know only English."

"Well, that's because there are 22 languages recognised by the Indian constitution. Apart from that there are hundreds of dialects. And you know Hari, it is believed that in India the dialect changes almost every twenty kilometres. Isn't it wonderful to have this kind of variety?"

"It sure is. And mum talking of variety the cultural programme presented by the students was awesome. The dances, the costumes, the music - I have never seen anything like this before. Wait till I tell my friends about it. They'll turn green."

"What did you like best Hari?" asked Varsha.

"Everything was wonderful. The Od...Odissi dance and the one with the sticks - what's it called?"

"Dandia."

"Ya, ya, Dandia, and then the one in which the dancers wore long skirts, brightly coloured masks with large eyes, Katha.......?"

"Kathakali."

"Yep, that's the one. And that dance Bhangra - what an infectious beat it had! I had to sit tight to hold myself back from getting up and dancing."

Manisha looked at Varsha and said, "You know Varsha the minute we landed in India Hari had started cribbing. He went on complaining about the crowds, the pollution, the filth, the noise and just about everything. He wanted to take the first flight back to New York."

"Is it true Hari?" Varsha asked in mock anger.

"Yep, ... my first impression of India was quite terrible."

"And what do you think of my country now that you have spent ten days here."

"Well, I must admit after spending time with all you lovely people my opinion has been turned on its head."

"Really?" asked Varsha.

"Yes dude, the respect you guys give to your elders, the tender relationship the grandparents share with their grandchildren, the amount of time the family spends together - it's all so....so amazing. There is so much bonding between family members. You share your joys, your sorrows, every little thing on a day-to-day basis - not merely on anniversaries and festivals," Hari paused and looked at Manisha who was staring at him in surprise. She had never heard him speak with so much passion about anything.

"And mum the culture of this place also fascinates me no end. The colourful costumes, the pulsating beats, the terrific dances - there is so much vibrancy, vitality and variety here," Hari said his eyes sparkling. He then turned to Varsha, "I should thank you for giving me a chance to enjoy all this."

Varsha got up and walking up to Hari took his hand in hers, "Hari, it is I who should thank you."

"Why?"

"Because I think I had started taking my family, my culture and my country for granted. Today you have made me realise how precious they all are."

"So, Hari when you landed you called India the pits. What do you have to say now?" asked Manisha.

"*Saare Jahan se achha, Hindustan hamara....*" Hari said as he and Varsha high-fived each other.

The Real Hero

"Sahil, my dad is going to be the chief guest at the Annual Sports meet," said Naresh, thumping Sahil on his back. Naresh's father R. Balasubramanian or Bala as he was popularly known, had played cricket for the country and his terrific performance had made him the heartthrob of millions.

"Look, here comes Vivek. Let's give him the good news," Sahil said. Vivek, Naresh and Sahil were VIII class students of Hyderabad Public School and the best of friends. "I know dude," Vivek said when Sahil told him. And guess who'll inaugurate the Annual Day on 15th March?"

"Who?" Naresh asked.

"My father! Who else?" Vivek's father Vikram Reddy was one of the top stars of Telugu cinema. Whenever Vikram uncle came to school, he would be mobbed by the students, the teachers and the office staff. That evening as Sahil trudged home, he felt a tad despondent. Not that he was jealous. But he did feel a tinge of envy.

Sahil's father Sudeep Naidu was a Colonel in the army. Sahil was proud of him but he wasn't a celebrity like Vikram uncle or Bala uncle. The teachers fell over themselves being nice to them and would keep asking them for favours, be it studio passes or pavilion passes. Sahil was an all-rounder, excelling in academics, sports and other activities. Yet he felt inferior to Naresh and Vivek. All because their fathers were celebrities while his father…

***

In May, war broke out and Colonel Sudeep Naidu was sent to Kargil. As the conflict raged on, for Sahil and his mother Maya, life revolved around the happenings on the front. Sahil would write one letter a day to his father and receive sporadic replies. Mother and son would be glued to every news bulletin.

On June 27th, Maya was informed that Colonel Naidu had led an assault on a vital peak in the Dras sector. The peak had been captured but 12 lives had been lost. The Colonel himself had been badly injured and was in the army hospital in Srinagar.

"H..how serious is… his con.. condition….?" Maya stammered unable to think clearly. "Can't say at the moment madam. Our doctors are trying their best. Colonel is a tough man… let's hope for the best."

Maya broke down as she related the conversation to Sahil.

Maya and Sahil decided to leave the very next day for Srinagar. Sahil went to the Principal Mr. O.N. Puri to seek his permission. He agreed but asked Sahil to spare some time to attend the school assembly in the morning.

The next day at nine, Sahil stood in the assembly, in his usual place between Naresh and Vikram. After the prayer, the principal addressed the gathering. "As you know fierce fighting is going on in the northern borders of our country. Our valiant soldiers are sacrificing their todays for our tomorrows. We are proud that among these real-life heroes is one who is part of our family. He led the attack on a key enemy position. Three bullets hit him but he fought on until the crucial peak was captured. That brave soldier, who is now battling for his life in the army hospital in Srinagar, is none other than Colonel Sudeep Naidu, father of our Sahil," Mr. Puri paused and looked at the sea of faces standing before him.

"Yesterday when I came to know that Sahil will be leaving today to meet his father, I thought he should carry with him the wishes of the entire school," he turned his gaze to the young student, "Sahil please come."

Sahil walked up to the dais. The principal handed him a huge rolled-up drawing sheet. As he unrolled it and looked at it, tears sprang into his eyes. It was a huge collage with scores of signatures, small sketches, lines of poetry, little paintings—all wishing Colonel Sudeep Naidu a quick recovery. "Yesterday our whole school spent the day making this for your father. From nursery to class twelve almost every student has contributed something here. Please tell Colonel Naidu our prayers are with him and his comrades," Mr. Puri said.

As Sahil walked home, he found it difficult to control his tears. The love his entire school had demonstrated and the pride he felt for his father were overwhelming.

***

When Sahil and his mother reached Srinagar, they were given some good news. "Colonel Naidu is well on his way to recovery. However, he is resting now. You can meet him tomorrow morning," the attending doctor told them. Sahil's father was in the ICU and they could get a glimpse of him from outside. He was lying swathed in bandages with a serene expression on his face.

The next day Colonel Naidu was shifted to the ward. Sahil rushed to meet him and held out his hand. He wanted to throw himself on his father and hug him, but he was scared of hurting him. He showed his father the poster.

"It is lovely. As lovely as your letters that kept me going," Colonel Naidu said kissing Sahil on his forehead.

***

After a couple of weeks, Colonel Naidu returned home to a tumultuous welcome. A month later, Hyderabad Public School, in collaboration with Cine Club, Hyderabad and Veteran Cricketers' Association, organised a charity cricket match.

The proceeds were to go to the family members of the Kargil martyrs. The captain of the Veteran Cricketers' Eleven was Bala while Vikram led the cine stars. The chief guest of the closing ceremony, who stole the limelight with his stirring speech, was Colonel Sudeep Naidu.

Patriotism

"Nanaji, what is patriotism?" asked Ajit.

"It means going to jail like Gandhiji and Chacha Nehru or dying for your country like Bhagat Singh," explained his sister Naina.

"Yes Naina, you are right. But it also means a lot more. To be a patriot one need not die or go to jail. One can show one's love for one's country in many small ways," Nanaji said.

"How?"

"By loving its culture and its people. Do you remember Ajit, on 26th after the Republic Day Parade a tune was being played?"

"Yes Nanaji, as soon as the tune started you stood and continued standing till the end."

"Do you know what the tune was?"

"I know, Nanaji," Naina said. "It was our national anthem – *Jana gana mana...*"

"Good. But do you know why I got up and stood to attention?"

"No, Nanaji. Why?"

"As a mark of respect to the national anthem. And unfortunately, I was the only one to do so. Your father continued to read the paper and your mother went on with her conversation on the phone. Earlier in the cinema halls, at the end of the movie, the national anthem was played. But it was found that the people used to leave the hall midway, laughing, shouting and creating a racket. The Government then decided to stop the playing of the national anthem. The reason why I gave you this example is to explain to you that a person's patriotism can be reflected in simple day to day things like his respect for his language, his nation's anthem or flag and above all the love for his fellow countrymen."

"Nanaji, I still don't understand. I thought patriotism was all about dying for one's country or making a big sacrifice."

"Yes Naina, you are right. It is about big things but also little ones too. And remember, it is not the battlefield alone which produces patriots. In the battlefield of life too you will find many martyrs. Okay, let me tell you a story which will help you understand better."

"Yayy Nanaji! Tell me a story about ghosts and vampires," shouted Ajit.

"No Ajit, I'll tell you a story about real people and their real problems. But not today; this Sunday, I'll take you for a picnic to a small village around 100 kms from here. We'll spend the day there and return by night."

***

On Sunday Nanaji, Naina and Ajit started very early on their 'picnic'. They took the first train to the village Hanumanpalli.

Two and half hours later they found themselves at a tiny and rather dusty railway station. They got down and stepped outside. A large well-built man wearing a white dhoti and kurta and sporting a huge turban greeted them with folded hands.

He led them to a bullock cart and much to Ajit's delight lifted and placed him on the cart. The cart trundled on for almost an hour till they finally reached the village. They alighted in front of a large brick house. An elderly man and woman came out, greeted nanaji and fussed over the kids. They spoke in a dialect which Naina and Ajit found difficult to understand.

An hour later, after they had their breakfast nanaji took them to a huge peepal tree where there was a platform. They sat down and nanaji started his story.

"Around ten years ago there was a young man whose name was Akash. He was studying to be a doctor. After he completed his

MBBS he worked hard and won a scholarship to USA. He got his masters degree and decided to come back. Along with him ten of his friends had also gone for higher studies to America. They all stayed back but Akash returned. Akash's father was not very happy with his son's decision. He was very proud that his son had got a foreign degree. He wanted his son to make America his home, earn a lot of money and finally invite his parents and sister also to settle down in America. But Akash was adamant.

'My country has spent lakhs of rupees on educating me. I have to repay this debt. The only way I can do it is by serving the people here. And moreover, India and its villages need good doctors far more than rich countries like America.'

"What finally happened Nanaji? Did Akash come back to India?"

"Yes child, he did. In the beginning he worked in a Government Hospital in the city. A year later an epidemic broke out in the nearby villages. When Akash learnt about that he just packed his bags and left. He didn't even inform his parents."

"Why?" asked Ajit.

"Because they would have stopped him, silly. I have read that during epidemics, sometimes the doctors who are treating the patients also die," Naina said.

"Yes, Naina is right. Anyways, a week later Akash's father got a postcard from him saying that he was busy treating the patients and that the situation was very grim. However, Akash did not mention where exactly he was fearing that his father would land up and try to drag him back. Two weeks later his father received a phone call saying that Akash had been admitted in the City Hospital in a serious condition.

His parents rushed to see him. He was in a very bad state. He could barely speak.

"Why are you torturing yourself, as well as us, son?" His father asked him while his mother started sobbing.

"I... I... can't help it father. I can't bear to see people suffer."

"Your friends are enjoying life in America, earning pots of money and look at you here – fighting for your life. I can't understand what you are getting by doing all this. If you don't care about yourself at least spare a thought for your poor mother. Just see her condition. She has gone half mad worrying about you."

"Father, I don't think I'll ever be able to convince you about my actions. All I can say is that I have the satisfaction that I have been able to save so many lives. Forgive me if I have tortured you. But... but please try to understand that I could not help it. I can't watch people dying all around me and not do anything."

After battling for a month Akash died in his mother's arms.

The entire village was there at his cremation and there was not even one eye which was dry.

The villagers decided to pay homage to Akash. They launched a drive to collect donations for building a small hospital in the village. They approached the local MLA who agreed to organise a hefty donation thinking that the hospital would be named after him. However, the villagers were adamant. They took the money, built the hospital and called Akash's parents for the opening ceremony. Akash's father inaugurated the hospital.

"Come, I want to show you something," Nanaji said and taking their hands in his he led them to a building a few hundred meters behind the peepal tree."

They stopped in front of a blue board.

"Naina, please read what is written."

"Akash Memorial Hospital – In memory of Dr. Akash Rai, who saved this village from death."

Naina looked at her grandfather. Nanaji's eyes were wet with tears.

"Nanaji, Akash Rai, but your surname is also Rai... was he your... ?"

"Yes, my child, he was my son. Your mother's elder brother. As a professor of Philosophy, I always thought I knew everything about everything. But my son taught me the true essence of the term 'service' and the real meaning of the word 'patriotism'."

Kabir

This is not a tale about 'once upon a time' it is a story set in the 'here and now'. The hero of the story is Kabir who lives in Dinapur a prosperous village in central India. Dinapur is situated between the towns of Sonipet and Minarganj. Kabir has no surname; in fact, he has no religion. No one knows whether he is a Muslim or a Hindu.

Dinapur has a Masjid and a Mandir which are next to each other, separated only by a narrow pathway. The Masjid is looked after by Mullah Hyder while the caretaker of the Mandir is Pandit Gopal Das. Many years ago, early one morning, the Mullah and the Pandit heard the cries of a little baby. They went out to investigate and found a three-month-old infant lying on the pathway crying. The Mullah and the Pandit looked at each other and then looked around.

"Whose child could this be?" the Pandit mumbled.

"Some unfortunate mother must have abandoned it?" the Mullah muttered.

"What do we do now?"

"I think we should give it refuge?"

"Yes, we cannot abandon it. After all it has been left on the door step of God."

"But who is to take it?" asked the Pandit.

"Good question. We don't even know whether he is a Muslim or a Hindu," the Mullah said picking up the child and examining it carefully for any hints that would help him solve the mystery.

The two of them kept pondering over the issue for sometime.

Dinapur was a village well known for its unity. Hindus and Muslims were in equal number and lived together peacefully.

During Diwali and Holi, the Muslims joined the celebration with enthusiasm and during Eid the Hindus never lagged behind in enjoying the festivities with their Muslim brothers.

Finally, the Mullah said, "Panditji does it really matter whether he is a Muslim or a Hindu. He is the child of God and let us treat him as one."

"You are absolutely right. He belongs to all of us. I think let us bring him up together. Let us also give him a name which is common to both religions."

"That is a good idea. Let us call him Kabir. After all no one knows the religion of Sant Kabir and he was equally loved by the Muslims and the Hindus."

"Wonderful. I will teach Kabir all the Hindu scriptures," the Pandit declared taking little Kabir in his arms.

"And I will teach him to recite the Quran Sharif," the Mullah said.

***

And so, Kabir grew up in the Masjid and the Mandir. If in the morning his breakfast would be the prasad in the temple, his lunch would be with the Mullah in the Mosque. One day he would sleep in the Masjid and the next day in the Mandir. Both the Mullah and the Pandit had no family and treated Kabir like their own son. He too had great love and respect for them. He learnt the Quran from the Mullah and the Bhagvat Geeta from the Pandit. He would perform namaaz in the Masjid and puja in the Mandir. The villagers too had accepted him as one of their own and being a fun-loving child, he was liked by all.

At the time when this story unfolds Kabir was a young lad of sixteen. He was tall and well built and a real asset to his guardians chachu Mullah and kaka Pandit. He would help them in maintaining the mosque and the temple. He would run errands for them and if any of them fell ill would tend to him like a son tending to his father. Every two months Kabir would be sent by his chachu and kaka to the town of Sonipet which was around thirty kilometres from Dinapur to pick up provisions and whatever else that was not available in the village.

Two days after Shivaratri, Kabir took the money from his kaka and chachu and went by bus to Sonipet. He finished his shopping and hitched a ride in a truck back to Dinapur. The truck dropped him on the main road, two kilometres away from the village. When he reached the outskirts of his village it was dark. In the horizon he could he could see a golden glow. Puzzled he quickened his steps. He saw a group of villagers running towards the main road. He recognised one of them and called out, "What happened Hariram? Where are you all going?"

Hariram came up to him panting. "Kabir, haven't you a heard? Riots have broken out in Minarganj. It seems a carcass of a cow was found in the Shiva temple which is on the outskirts of the town. The Hindus, suspecting that it was the handiwork of Muslims, reacted immediately and plundered two Mosques in Minarganj. An hour later our village was attacked by both Muslim and Hindu mobs. A few houses were burnt and some villagers hurt. The mobs then fought with each other for sometime and then left, possibly to return with reinforcements. It is not safe to be here. That is why we are leaving for Sonipet. It seems it is peaceful there."

"I am coming from Sonipet and I had no idea about this madness. What about our Masjid and Mandir?"

"I think Mullah Haider and Panditji are still there."

"Then I better rush," Kabir said and started running.

"Wait, Kabir, don't go there. Mandir and Masjid will be the first targets when the mobs return. It is madness to go back to the village."

"I can't leave my chachu and kaka in trouble, Hariram," Kabir shouted and dumping the bags in his hand in a nearby bush he ran as fast as possible in the direction of the Mandir and Masjid.

When he reached the Masjid, it was quiet all around. The silence was eerie. The door was shut.

Kabir banged on the door. There was no response. He banged harder and shouted, "Chachu, it is me, Kabir."

After a few agonising moments the door opened a few inches and chachu poked his head out. Kabir had never seen him so scared.

"Kabir beta quickly come in," he said dragging Kabir by his arm and shutting the door. Kabir followed him. In the courtyard he could see at least fifty women and children huddled together.

"What's all this?"

Chachu sat down on a cot with his head in his hands. "I have been living in this village now for 40 years but I have never seen this kind of insanity. Some of the men have been hurt, some have even joined the mob. Some have left to go and get help. I gathered as many children and women as I could and brought them here. Thank God beta you are safe, I was so worried."

"How is kaka?" Kabir asked.

"I have no idea," chachu said.

"I'll go and have a look."

"You stay put. If the fanatics return you will be chopped to pieces. At least inside the Masjid we are safe."

"Then let me go and bring kaka here?"

"Are you mad? If the Muslims come to know we have given shelter to a Hindu they'll butcher all of us."

"Then why are you giving me shelter? I too am not a Muslim?" Kabir said looking straight at chachu.

"You are one of us," chachu replied avoiding Kabir's gaze.

Kabir quietly got up and walked out of the Masjid.

He went next door to the Mandir. The story was almost the same except that there was no one else with kaka in the Mandir.

"Beta, I am so relieved that you are okay."

"Kaka, why didn't you leave?"

"How could I leave my *bhagwan* and go Kabir."

"What if the mob comes back?"

"I'll face it. I'll die if I have to."

"Chachu has given shelter to some women and children. In case Hindus attack the Masjid, we will have to give them shelter in the temple."

"We can't Kabir. If Hindus come to know we have given shelter to Muslims they won't spare us."

"But Kaka I too am not a Hindu? You should drive me out of here."

No beta, you are like my son, you are not a Muslim," Kaka said.

Just then they could hear someone banging on the door.

"Open up, you infidel."

"We know you are hiding like a rat inside." They could hear several shouts.

Kabir sprang forward.

"What are you doing?" Kaka shouted holding his arm.

"Kaka, I have to face them. Or they will burn down the temple."

Wrenching his arm free he ran towards the door. He opened it and stepped out.

Outside it was quite dark. He could make out a crowd of more than twenty men. They had sticks, swords and daggers in their hands.

"Catch him and butcher the infidel."

"Don't leave the pig alone."

"We'll scatter his pieces in the Mandir and then set fire to it." The angry screams echoed in the still night air as the men surged forward.

"Wait." Kabir shouted his voice rising above the din. "Will you butcher a man of your own community?"

"What do you mean?"

"Are you a Muslim?"

"Of course, I am."

"He is lying."

"I can prove it," replied Kabir and slowly began reciting the *Surah Fateh* from the Quran. Kabir had learnt the beautiful verse in praise of Allah, from chachu. As he recited each word perfectly the crowd stepped back.

"Okay we are convinced you are a Muslim. Now get out of the way and allow us to burn this place down."

"I won't allow it."

"Why? You are a Muslim - this Mandir should hold no value for you."

"It does. It is the abode of God, just like a Masjid."

"Get out, or I'll chop your head off," shouted a tall and burly fellow advancing.

"You can't kill me. I am not only a Muslim; my guardian is Mullah Hyder the mullah of the Masjid next door. If you shed my blood you will rot in hell."

The men looked at each other uncertainly. "Come on, let us leave this madcap and look for some Hindu houses to destroy," one of them snapped and the crowd turned and vanished.

Kabir went in and told Kaka what had transpired.

"My son, I will forever be grateful to you for saving my *bhagwan* and his abode."

"Don't forget Kaka, he is my *bhagwan* too," Kabir said.

***

Ten minutes later Kabir went to the Masjid carrying some provisions from the Mandir.

"Here Chachu, I have got something for all of you to eat." He then related to chachu his encounter with the Muslim mob.

"*Jai Shri Ram*," suddenly the still night air was shattered by strident cries. Chachu went to the window and tried to see through a crack in the pane.

He came back shaking with fear. "There are more than fifty Hindus with *trishul*s in their hands shouting and screaming. I think we are gone. They will cut all of us to pieces."

Asking everyone to stay in the shadows Kabir opened the door and boldly stepped out.

"Kill the traitor, kill him."

"You can't kill me. I am a Hindu."

"You coward, you are lying to protect your skin."

"Get him."

Three pairs of hands grabbed him and a *trishul* was placed on his throat.

Kabir started chanting the *Gayatri Mantra*, which he had learnt from his Kaka. As his strong and clear voice rose above the din one by one his captors released him.

"Now get out of the way. We have come to destroy this Masjid. We will lay the foundation stone of a Mandir today itself. *Jai Shri Ram!*"

"I will not allow you to do it?"

"Why? If they can defile our temples, why shouldn't we destroy their mosques?"

"Whether it is a mosque or a temple it is the abode of God and you can destroy it only over my dead body."

"Then be prepared to die," roared one of them.

"If you kill me, God will never spare you. My guardian is Pandit Gopal Das, the priest of the temple."

The attackers looked at each other. "We can't kill a high-class brahmin even if he is a supporter of Muslims," one of them mumbled. They turned around and ran in search of another quarry screaming *"Jai Shri Ram."*

***

By early next morning the police pickets had been posted in Dinapur and the residents had started returning to the village.

In the evening a meeting of all the important people in the village was called by Pandit Gopal Das and Mullah Hyder. Pandit Gopal Das was the first to address the gathering. "Friends, what has happened in the last two days has been shocking. Our village has always been a symbol of unity. But this fabric of unity was destroyed by one single gust of communal breeze. We have always lived like brothers. But just in a few hours we became strangers and yes, in a few cases, even enemies. A handful of fanatics were ready to make us forget our years of love and bonding. In this hour of madness there was only one sane voice. And Hyder bhai will tell you about that voice."

"Panditji is absolutely right. This madness that gripped the village did not spare even Panditji and me. We, who are servants of God, who are supposed to preach brotherhood and faith, started thinking in terms of Hindus and Muslims. Our Masjid and the Mandir would have been destroyed and the Hindus and Muslims would have lived and died like sworn enemies but for one person. He is not a sadhu or a mullah, he is neither a leader nor a *goonda*. He is a sixteen-year-old boy who values our unity more than his life. His name, as you must have guessed, is Kabir."

Mullah Hyder then went on to narrate the incidents of the

previous night and how Kabir had risked his life to save the Masjid and the Mandir.

Mullah Hyder sat down. Panditji got up and started speaking. "I think Kabir has taught us a very important lesson. If we are united then no one can touch us. If Kabir alone could stand up to so many thugs just think had we all faced them together, would they have been able to even touch our village. Just as Sant Kabir brought together the Hindus and Muslims the modern Kabir too has shown us the path of unity. Now it is up to us to follow his example."

The words of Mullah Hyder and Pandit Gopal Das left a lasting impression on the villagers. The Hindus and Muslims took a pledge to live like members of one family. Every attempt to create differences between the communities failed. Today Dinapur is no more known as Dinapur it is called Ektapur - the abode of unity.

The Promise

"Papa, why is mum crying?" Aniket asked his father Raj Singh.

"Son, I have to go back on duty." Raj Singh was a Captain in the Indian Army.

"But Papa, you came back just yesterday after more than six months."

"Can't help it Ani. I got the message this morning from the head quarters."

"Where do you have to go?"

"Pakistani intruders have invaded Kargil. I have to go there."

"Where is Kargil, Papa?"

"It is to the extreme north of the country - on the Indo-Pak border. We have been taken by surprise and have to fight back."

"When will you come back?"

"I can't say, beta. It might take a few weeks...or a few months...or..."

"But Papa, you have to be here on 4th July."

"Why son?"

"Come on Papa, don't tell me you have forgotten my birthday. I am going to be ten this year. And you promised that we shall have a special celebration."

"I am really sorry Ani. I completely forgot." Raj Singh pulled his son close and hugged him. "I'll definitely be back for your birthday."

"Promise," Ani held out his hand.

"Promise," his father took his hand in his and shook it.

***

That was a month ago. The last four weeks had gone by in a haze of images - cold, bitter and hard. Raj Singh's regiment had been in the thick of battle for the last ten days. They had met with partial success but had also paid a heavy price for it. The enemy was firmly entrenched in bunkers on top of the mountain. The intruders were better clothed, better equipped and had the distinct advantage of height. All this had made them seemingly unassailable at first. However, braving the icy cold conditions and inching up the steep gradient, Raj Singh and his brave men had made strike after strike. They had captured two peaks and lost twelve men. Today was the final assault on the most crucial of enemy stations - Point 3443.

The intrepid soldiers moved forward groping for footholds. It was pitch dark and all around there was an inky blankness. The enemy perched on top was firing every few minutes. Raj Singh was sure the intruders had little idea of their whereabouts. They were just firing blindly in the hope of striking.

"Baldev, Sukhbir, Haneef you come with me. We'll circle the peak and try to attack them from behind. Jaswant, you take the rest and go ahead," Raj Singh barked his orders and set off followed by his men. They knew they had to be extremely careful in circling the peak - one small miss and they would fall in the gorge below.

As they moved ahead, Raj Singh noticed there was a lull in firing.

"I think they assume that we have given up for the night," he whispered to Haneef. "This is the ideal time. Let us try to reach the top as fast as possible."

They started crawling up. Just as they reached the top, they saw shadows looming ahead. The intruders had not relaxed, rather they had been waiting for Raj Singh and his men to come up.

Realising they had been trapped Raj Singh yelled, "Fire."

The booming of the guns shattered the stillness of the night.

Silhouetted against the light of the marching gun fire he could make out at least twenty-five intruders. As he rolled on the ground firing away, he hoped Jaswant and his men would soon reach. From the corner of his eyes, he saw Haneef gun down four men and then collapse as three bullets hit him. Raj Singh fired and as usual was bang on target. Two intruders came hurtling down the slopes and fell into the gorge below. Just then he heard shots from the other side and he realised with relief that Jaswant and his men had reached. But he knew even this wouldn't be enough. From inside the bunkers the intruders seemed to be crawling out like ants. Raj Singh and his men were outnumbered 1 to 5. Shouting words of encouragement, he continued moving.

The next half an hour was like a scene from the numerous war movies he had seen as a child. Everything seemed to be happening all at once. The ricocheting of gun fire, shouts of triumph, shrieks of pain it was like a crazy nightmare. Suddenly a bullet ripped into his shoulder almost tearing it apart. But Raj Singh was oblivious to the pain. His only concern was to annihilate the enemy and capture the peak. The enemy caught between the two squads was taken by surprise. The confusion made the intruders sitting ducks for sometime. Raj Singh and his men capitalised on that. But soon the intruders regained their composure and fought back.

After a few minutes there was complete silence on the other side. Jaswant and his men had probably died fighting. Raj Singh could see neither Baldev nor Sukhbir. He was all alone.

He looked towards the bunker. Five shadows were moving towards him stealthily. He knew the minute he fired they would know his position and finish him in an instant. He had to distract them. He looked around. Just beside him was a body of an intruder. He lifted it and with great difficulty crawled under it. The body was heavy and it needed a great effort to raise it. However, Raj Singh knew this was the only way he had hope of getting at the enemy. He also had to be careful. Any movement and that would be the end of Captain Raj Singh. He would love dying for his country but not like this with his mission unaccomplished.

He got under the body and adjusted himself in such a way that only the snout of his rifle would be visible from above and that too only in the light of the gunfire. He waited with bated breath. The soldiers moved forward stealthily. When they were within striking range he fired - one, two, three shots and then the fourth one. He watched them slump. Two bullets thudded into the body which covered Raj Singh. The fifth man realising where his enemy was shot at him. The bullets whizzed past. He couldn't see the soldier. He seemed to have disappeared. Cautiously Raj Singh dislodged the body and stood up. Just then a shadow lunged at him. The Captainwent sprawling with his assailant on top. Raj Singh lashed out with his rifle's bayonet. There was a long agonising shriek and his opponent slumped forward. Raj Singh didn't have the strength to even withdraw his rifle.

He didn't know how long he stayed like that. After what seemed an eternity, he tried getting up and fell down instantly. He then decided to crawl towards the bunker which was a hundred feet away. As he slowly inched forward, he looked around for any sign of any movement. Finally on reaching the bunker he removed a tiny Indian flag from his shirt pocket and struck it on the ground. He raised his hand in salute and with 'Jai Hind' on his lips collapsed.

***

Aniket's mother Kavita was listening to the evening news on TV.

"We have just received an update on the situation in Kargil. The Rajputana Rifles have captured Point - 3443. However, in that process eight of our brave soldiers have laid down their lives. The martyrs who were led by Major Raj Singh killed more than thirty five enemy intruders and sacrificed their lives for their country....."

Kavita felt her body turn icy cold. 'No...it couldn't be...this couldn't' happen to Raj'. She started sobbing uncontrollably.

"Mum, what happened, please tell me..." Aniket was shaking her.

She stared at him red eyed, unable to speak.

***

"Mum, there is some mistake," Aniket was telling her. It was past midnight. They had been listening to the evening news bulletin. Kavita had telephoned the head quarters. It was true. Although they had not located his body it was clear that he had died. All the other bodies had been found except his. His body had most likely fallen into the gorge below the treacherous peak. That is why they had not announced that the brave Captain was missing in action but had declared him dead.

Aniket refused to believe that his father was dead.

"They haven't recovered his....his.. body Mum, that means he is alive. Don't forget he promised that he would come on my birthday. Papa never breaks his promise. Tomorrow is 4th July and he will definitely come. Papa is an Indian soldier and our soldiers always keep their word."

Kavita pulled him close and hugged him tears streaming down her face. How she wished her son's words would come true.

***

On 4th July Aniket woke up early and got dressed. His Papa would be coming today and he wanted to be ready to receive him. Kavita watched him silently unable to stem her flow of tears. In the last twenty-four hours condolence messages had been pouring in from all over the country. Raj Singh had become a national hero. The capture of Point 3443 was a decisive step, the first major breakthrough the Indian forces had made since the intrusion.

The whole day Aniket kept looking out of the window. By evening sadness, like the lengthening shadows of the day, started creeping across his face. At eleven he dozed off by the window sill out of sheer exhaustion. He didn't know how long he slept. He suddenly woke up with a start. Someone had rung the door bell. He dashed out of his room towards the front door and yanked it open.

Outside in the dark he could see a tall figure in the shadows. The night sky was cloudy. But Aniket needed neither the moon nor the stars to recognise his father.

"Papa," he screamed rushing forward and hugging him. Raj Singh bend down and kissed his face. But he didn't enclose him in a bear hug as he always did. Aniket looked up and it was then that he noticed. Papa's both arms were in a sling.

***

Ten minutes later the three of them were sitting in the living room. Aniket was on his father's lap and Kavita near his feet looking up at him. The army jeep which had come to drop Raj Singh had been sent away.

"After hoisting the little flag, I passed out. I don't remember how long I lay there. I think it was the pain in my shoulders which woke me. I started crawling down slowly. I knew it was impossible for me to reach the base camp on my own. I only wanted to try staying alive till the army patrol reached me. As I inched forward, I lost balance and slid down. I thought I was gone. I was heading straight for the gorge. Fortunately, I landed on the thick branches of a tree which was growing outward from a ledge. The tree broke my fall. I managed to slowly move on to the ledge. I lay there on the tiny ledge, 8000 feet above the ground, close to twenty-four hours. I could feel the life ebb out slowly. I had accomplished my mission. We had captured Point 3443 but I would probably fail in keeping my word to my son. I knew I had to fight death... till the very last...after all how could I break my promise to my little Field Marshal waiting for me at home....

I was luckily spotted by an aircraft patrolling above and rescued. At the base camp I told everyone to keep the fact that I was alive a secret. I wanted to see the sparkle in your eyes and the expressions of delight on your faces when I stood before you."

"I had given up hope, but Ani hadn't. He was sure his Papa would keep his promise," Kavita said.

Aniket threw his arms around his Papa and Raj Singh kissed his tear-stained face.

Time Pass Uncle

"*Time pass chana-phalli,*" Hari heard the all-familiar booming voice as he stepped out of the school gate.

"Nampalli, Lingampalli, Kukatpalli, Marrepalli, *time pass chana-phalli,*" the voice rose above the din. Hari ran towards the owner of the voice.

"Time Pass Uncle!"

"Hari beta, I was looking for you," replied Shauqat Ali. Hari's Time Pass Uncle.

Shauqat Ali sold *chana* (gram) and *phalli* (groundnuts) on his cycle. On the stand was fixed a huge basket divided into six compartments. Each compartment contained a tasty mixture of a different flavour. By adding various spices to the *chana* and *phalli* Shauqat Ali made several mouth-watering 'items' as he called them. But more than his 'items' Hari liked his style. He was very tall and burly with a thick beard and a booming voice. Every afternoon when the school closed he would appear at the school gates and start advertising his wares in his classic style: "*Time Pass chana phalli.....*

Hari had nicknamed him Time Pass Uncle and soon all his friends called him that. Time Pass Uncle was very fond of Hari. Every day Hari would buy two rupees worth of 'mixture' from him and chat with his favourite uncle while munching it. Hari's school closed at 3.45 in the afternoon while his bus came at 4. For fifteen minutes daily Hari and Time Pass Uncle would gossip. Hari would tell him about his day at school, his friends and his teachers. Time Pass Uncle would tell him about his customers and anything interesting that he happened to see while going on his rounds.

Hari lived in a lane close to Charminar in Hyderabad. His father Narasimha Reddy was a rickshaw puller while his mother Parvati was a maidservant. He was a class six student and since he studied in a Government High School, his education was free.

"Why were you looking for me Uncle? Anything special?"

"You bet. Today I have made a brand-new mixture and can you guess what I have named it?"

Another special feature of Time Pass Uncle's 'dishes' was the unique name he gave to each one.

Hari shook his head.

"I have called my latest creation 'KBC Special'."

"Kaun Banega Crorepati Special?"*

"Yes."

"Will I become a crorepati if I sample your KBC special?" Hari asked grinning.

"No, but you will definitely feel like a crorepati once you taste it? Here taste my KBC special and tell me how terrific it is," Time Pass Uncle said handing him a paper packet.

"But Uncle I can't take your special today?"

"Why? Your stomach is upset, you have ulcers in your mouth, you are fasting?"

"No, no," Hari said looking down. "I d...don't have the money. My father has been suffering from fever for the last two days and has not gone to work."

"Come on, Hari beta. Who is asking for money now? Eat and enjoy. You can pay me later. And even if you don't, I won't really mind. We are friends, aren't we?" Time Pass Uncle said extending his large hand. Hari took the packet. "Thanks Uncle."

He popped the mixture in his mouth and exclaimed, "Wah Uncle! *Mast* hai!! I have not eaten anything so tasty in my life."

"Here have some more," Time Pass Uncle said grinning from ear to eat.

***

A few weeks later Hari's maternal grandmother amamma came to stay with them. She was very fond of Hari and he would spend most of his time with her.

"You know, Amamma today Time Pass Uncle made another special mixture. He has named it 'Super Sachin' and it is really super."

"Time Pass Uncle! What a strange name."

"I have given him that name. His actual name is Shauqat Ali."

"What! He is a Muslim!"

"Yes."

"But Hari you should not eat anything given by a Muslim. "

"Why Amamma?"

"They cannot be trusted. He might poison you or put some drugs into his mixture and get you addicted."

"Come on, Amamma. He is my friend. How can you even think of such a thing?"

"I can never trust a Muslim. I forbid you to eat what he sells."

"I don't care what you think. Time Pass Uncle is my friend and I will eat what he gives."

"Then I'll tell your parents to stop you," Amamma said and getting up walked away in a huff.

A few days later amamma went back to Barkatpura where she stayed with her eldest son.

That evening Hari told his mother Parvati about amamma's views about Time Pass Uncle.

"Amamma told me. I don't agree with what she says. But you should know the reason why she thinks so. When my younger brother, your mama Yadgiri, was fifteen years old there was a riot in Karimnagar. He and two of his friends were returning home when they were chased by group of Muslims and stabbed. He died on the spot. We could not even get his body. Since that day Amamma doesn't trust Muslims - she hates them."

"But ma, Time Pass Uncle is not like that. He is very fond of me."

"I know son. That is why I am not stopping you. I believe that neither are all Muslims bad nor all Hindus good."

***

Six months later Hari and his parents were sleeping in their one room house when there was a loud noise. Hari woke up with a start. Someone was banging the door. Narasimha opened the door. It was his friend Surya. He looked excited.

"Narasimha, there is a riot. Someone threw a petrol bomb in the Masjid. Muslims are out on the streets. Take everyone and escape as fast as you can?"

"But where do I go?"

"Go to Nampally station. In such times it is a far safer place then either houses or streets."

Within ten minutes Narasimha was driving his rickshaw at a feverish pace in the lanes and by lanes of Charminar. Hari and Parvati were huddled inside the rickshaw and the curtain was drawn. Hari was terrified. He had never been this scared in his life. He clung to his mother as they were knocked from side to side, every time the rickshaw took a sudden turn.

"Hey you!" He heard a shout.

The rickshaw braked to a halt, sending Hari lurching forward. He pulled the curtain aside and poked his head out. It was pitch dark outside. He could make out a tall, well-built man. In his hand was a long knife.

"You *kafir*! I'll first chop your head off and then take your rickshaw," the giant growled and sprang forward.

"Time Pass Uncle," Hari screamed and before Parvati could stop him jumped out.

The giant froze for a few seconds and then lumbered forward.

"Whaaat...Hari....Is it you?"

"Y...yes Uncle. This is my father and my mother is inside."

Shauqat Ali looked at Hari and then Narasimha.

"Get into the rickshaw. Quick," he snapped at Narasimha.

"B..but."

"There is no time to argue. A mob is coming this side. The three of you will be butchered. Get in and stay quiet."

Narasimha and Hari squeezed into the rickshaw.

Shauqat Ali climbed on to the three-wheeler and started pedaling furiously.

After around ten minutes they could hear shouting, screaming and sounds of doors and windows breaking.

"Shauqat *mian*. So you managed a rickshaw," they heard a shout.

"Yes, Afzal bhai. Though I would have preferred an auto, something is better than nothing."

Hari could not remember how long he sat cramped in the rickshaw. It seemed like hours. Finally, the rickshaw stopped.

"Come out," Shauqat said.

Narasimha jumped down and helped his wife and son out.

They were in a wide lane, lined by shops on either side.

Shauqat Ali walked a few steps and stopped in front of a shop. He bent down, unlocked the shutter and pulled it up. "This is my uncle's shop. Right now, he is using it only as a store. You are safe here. I will be locking the shop from outside. Till I come stay put."

He shepherded then inside, took the rickshaw in and after pulling down the shutter left.

Hari looked around. It was quite a large room. A number of boxes were lying around.

They sat huddled together. Hari did not realise when he fell asleep. When he woke up it was morning. The sunlight was filtering through the ventilator.

After sometime the shutter was pulled up. Shauqat Ali entered and pulled the shutter down. He was carrying a cloth bag.

"I have brought something to eat for you. It is not much, but that is all I could get. There is curfew in the city." He left a few minutes later after pulling down the shutter.

The whole day the three of them sat quietly waiting for Shauqat Ali to come.

He appeared in the evening after dark.

"The curfew has been relaxed for two hours. You can go now?"

"Is it safe to go home?"

"To Charminar?"

"Yes."

"No. That is where it all began. Don't you have relatives elsewhere in the city?"

"My brother lives in Barkatpura," Parvati said.

"Yes, that place will be safe. Go as quickly as you can. You have to reach before the curfew is lifted," Shauqat Ali said.

Hari and Parvati got into the rickshaw and Narasimha wheeled the Rickshaw out.

"Shauqat bhai, I don't know how to thank you. You saved our lives," Parvati said.

"You are calling me bhai and then thanking me. Does a sister have to thank her brother?" Shauqat said looking at Parvati. "If Hari had not called me, I would probably have killed Narasimha. I had a son; his name was Rahmat. He was Hari's age when he died."

"H...how did he die?"

"There was a Hindu-Muslim riot in Hyderabad. My father was coming out of the Masjid with Rahmat when a mob attacked it. My father and son both were killed by Hindus," Shauqat said and after patting Hari on his cheek turned and walked back.

*Kaun Banega Crorepati (also simply known as KBC) is an Indian Hindi-language television game show. It is the official Hindi adaptation of the 'Who Wants to Be a Millionaire'? franchise.

About the Author

Ramendra Kumar

Ramendra Kumar (Ramen) is an award-winning writer, Performance Storyteller and Inspirational Speaker with 43 books. His writings have been translated into 30 languages and have found a place in several textbooks and anthologies. His picture books published by NBT, India have been included in the Government of India's 'Samagra Shiksha' programme and have notched up sales of more than 2.5 lakh copies.

Ramen has been invited to many international literary festivals as well as Indian events such as Jaipur Litfest. His stories have been showcased by audio streaming apps including Spotify, Google, Apple Podcast, Talking Stories (London) etc. He has a page devoted to him on Wikipedia.

An alumnus of Hyderabad Public School, Begumpet, Ramen is an Engineer & an MBA. He was General Manager (Corporate Communications), Rourkela Steel Plant, when he took Voluntary Retirement to pursue his passions, in 2020. Ramen is now a Cancer Warrior and is undergoing treatment.

www.ingramcontent.com/pod-product-compliance
Lightning Source LLC
LaVergne TN
LVHW041636070526
838199LV00052B/3397